HOUGHTON MIFFLIN COMPANY BOSTON 1991

Smith. Barry. 1934-
A child's guide to bad behavior / Barry Smith. --
1st American ed. p.   cm.
Summary: Captioned illustrations depict the many
ways in which a child can misbehave.
ISBN 0-395-57435-8
1. Children -- Conduct of life -- Juvenile literature. 2.
Conduct disorders in children -- Juvenile literature.
(1. Behavior.)
I. Title.
HQ781.5.S65   1991
305.23 -- dc20   91-6596
                                              CIP
                                              AC

Designed by Janet James

First American edition 1991
Originally published in Great Britain in 1991 by
Pavilion Books Ltd.

Printed in Belgium

10 9 8 7 6 5 4 3 2 1

Sing and shriek

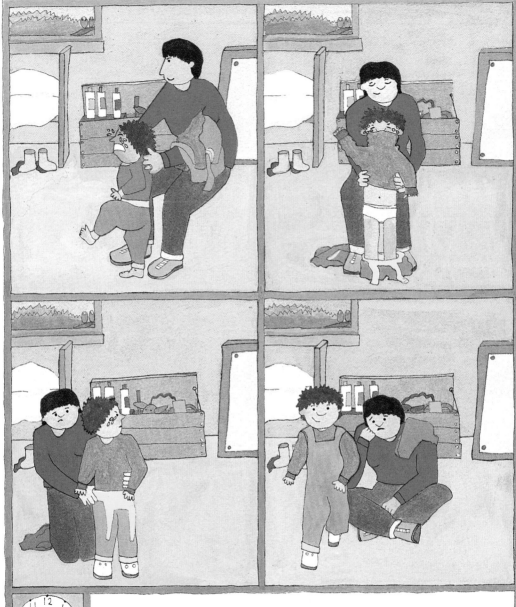

Whine and wail

Suddenly scribble

Breakfast brawl

and kitchen chaos

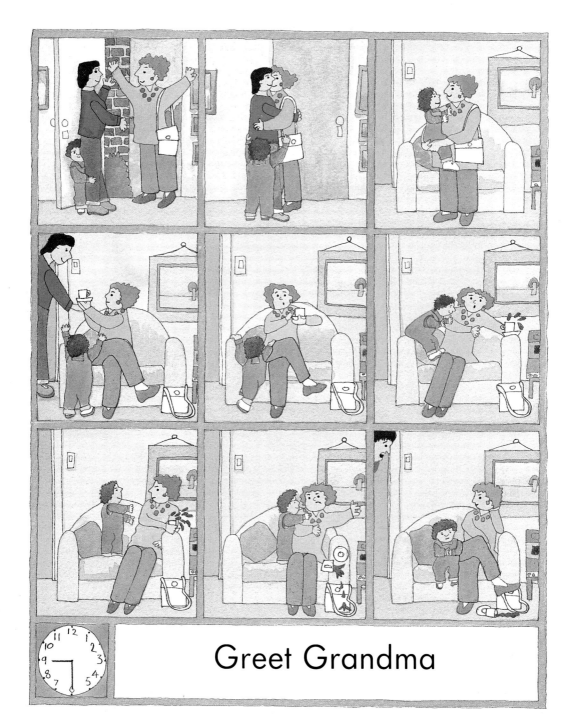

Greet Grandma

Play with her purse

Crush the cake

and pick at the pastries

Make Mom mad

Stamp and splash

Drop the display

and crash into the cartons

Make Mom mad and mean

Leave her lovely lunch

Games in the garden

and scary scenes near the shed

Shut with a slam

Temper, temper!

Push past people

and run around rioting

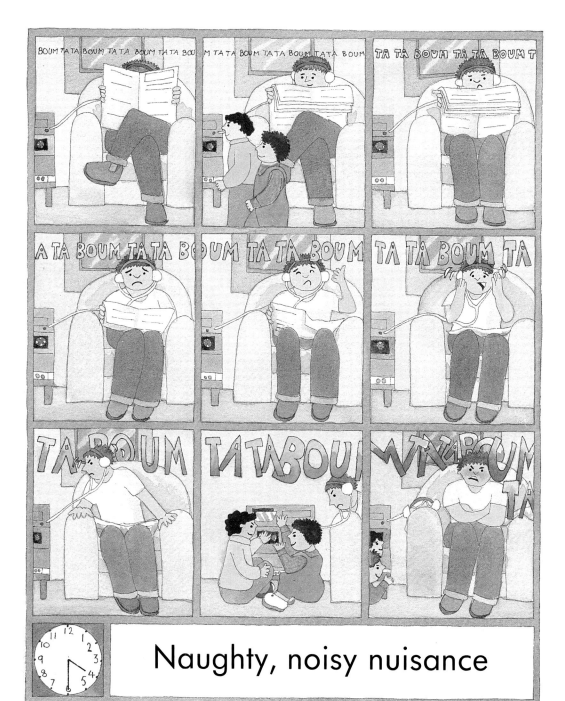

Naughty, noisy nuisance

Silly supper-time squabbles

Beasts in the bath

with weapons of water

Pyjama protest

Bedtime bother

Spoil the story

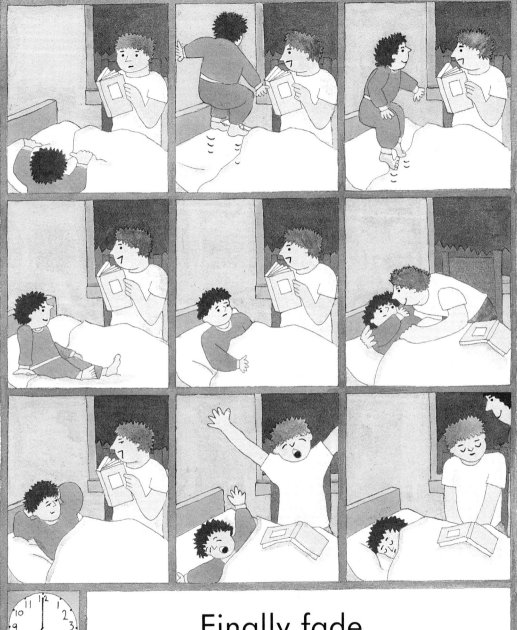

Finally fade . . .

into silence and sleep